The Little Book of
GIRL'S
FAIRY TALES

© 2012 Alligator Books Limited

Published in 2012 by
Alligator Books Limited,
Gadd House, Arcadia Avenue,
London N3 2JU.

11098
Printed in India.

The Little Book of Girl's Fairy Tales

Contents

Goldilocks and the Three Bears

Once upon a time, there lived a mischievous little girl called Goldilocks. She had beautiful curly blonde hair, as you might have guessed from her name.

Now Goldilocks lived near a forest, a forest that was thick with trees and beautiful flowers. All sorts of amazing creatures lived there too, like squirrels and rabbits and birds. Goldilocks loved to take long walks in the forest, exploring a different part every time.

One day, on one of her walks, Goldilocks came across a pretty cottage that she had never seen before. Little did she know that this particular cottage belonged to a family – the three Bears. There was a very big Papa Bear, a medium-sized Mama Bear and a very small Baby Bear.

Curious about who lived there, the little girl tapped on the door and waited for a reply. No one answered. Goldilocks tapped again, this time a little harder. Still there was no reply. Her curiosity soon got the better of her, and Goldilocks couldn't see the harm in turning the door handle, and peeping inside just for a moment.

But Goldilocks did more than just peep inside – she walked straight in! The cottage was empty, as the Bear family had gone out for a short walk while their porridge cooled on the kitchen table.

The little girl found herself in the Bears' sitting room, where she saw a picture of the family above the fireplace. There was Papa Bear, Mama Bear and Baby Bear.

Then the smell of something sweet began to waft through the air. The tasty aroma lured Goldilocks into the kitchen.

There she found three bowls of porridge set neatly on the table,

each with a spoon by its side. A rather large cat lay snoozing on the big chair.

"Hmmm," she said, "I'm quite hungry after my walk." Goldilocks began to wish the family who lived there would return and invite her to share their porridge. But although she looked everywhere, even under the table and in the cupboards, she could find no one. Goldilocks could resist the warm, sweet smell of porridge no longer, and made up her mind to taste just one spoonful.

The porridge was in three bowls – a very big bowl for the very big bear, a middle-sized bowl for the middle-sized bear, and a tiny bowl for the tiny bear. Goldilocks picked up the spoon next to the biggest bowl. For some reason, it didn't enter her head that she shouldn't eat someone else's breakfast, and that the family who lived there could return at any moment!

"This porridge is too hot!" she gasped. So Goldilocks moved to the middle-sized bowl. "This porridge is too cold."

Then Goldilocks moved to the third bowl, the very small one, and started to eat. "Mmmm, this porridge is just right," she said, and ate it all up without thinking!

When Goldilocks had finished the porridge, she returned to the sitting room and noticed three chairs. One was a very big chair, and she climbed on it and sat down. Oh dear! How hard it was! She was sure she could not sit there for long, so she climbed on the next, which was the middle-sized chair, but that was too soft for her liking.

Finally, Goldilocks tried the very small chair, and that one suited her just fine. But, if truth be told, Goldilocks was a bit too big for this chair, and the longer she sat there, the more the seat started to sink. Then it sank some more. Then, all of a sudden, the seat went 'pop' and fell out beneath her! Goldilocks had broken Baby Bear's chair!

The little girl pulled herself up and out of the broken chair,
wondering what she should do next. She noticed a staircase, which
sparked her curiosity once more. Up the stairs Goldilocks went,
tip-toeing step by step.

At the top of the stairs was a big yellow bedroom, and it was
the funniest-looking bedroom she had ever seen. Against the far
wall stood three well-made beds all in a row. In the middle was a
very big bed with a blue frame and a blue quilt. On one side of it
was a middle-sized bed with a pink frame and a pink quilt, and on
the other side was a very small bed with an orange frame and a

very cozy looking yellow and blue quilt.

Now, having eaten all of Baby Bear's porridge, Goldilocks felt ever so full and she soon began to feel rather sleepy. In fact, she became so sleepy that she decided to take a short nap.

First, Goldilocks tried the very big bed. "This bed is far too hard!" she gasped.

Then Goldilocks tried the middle-sized bed, but she sank right down into the mattress, "This one is far too soft."

Then she tried the very small bed – it was just right!

11

She cheekily moved the bed close to the window so she could watch the birds in the trees outside. Then Goldilocks climbed on the bed. She laid her head on Baby Bear's perfectly soft pillow, and she snuggled under Baby Bear's perfectly soft blanket. She even cuddled one of Baby's favourite teddy bears!

Baby Bear's bed was very, very comfy and within minutes Goldilocks fell into a deep, deep sleep. So deep, in fact, that she didn't hear the Bears come home.

As the Bear family trundled up the path to their house, refreshed from their morning walk and quite ready for their porridge, they had no idea what was awaiting them inside.

Papa Bear saw the first clue that something wasn't right when he noticed the front door was open. The Bears slowly entered their house, not knowing quite what to expect.

The Bears couldn't believe it! How cross Papa Bear was when he saw his spoon had been used and tossed to one side.

"Someone's been eating my porridge!" shouted Papa Bear ever so loudly.

"And someone's been eating MY porridge," shouted Mama Bear, not quite so loudly.

Then it was Baby Bear's turn: "Someone's been eating MY porridge… and they've eaten it all up!" he cried, as tiny tears dribbled down his furry cheeks.

The Bears wandered around the house looking for anything else that might be out of place. Papa Bear was also on the lookout in case the intruder was still there, hiding! They just couldn't believe that somebody had been in their home. The cat woke up from his nap and he could not believe it either!

The Bears went into the sitting room, where the very big Papa Bear bent to sit down in his very big chair. He announced in his very big voice, "Someone's been sitting in my chair!"

The medium-sized Mama Bear sat in her chair and gasped, "Someone's been sitting in MY chair, too! The cushions are all out of place, and they feel a bit warm!"

Then the very small Baby Bear squealed, "Oh, no! Someone's been sitting in MY chair, and they've broken it! My chair's nothing but a pile of wooden sticks!"

Poor Baby Bear was quite angry that his chair had been broken. In fact, all the Bears were starting to get cross and the more they saw, the crosser they got!

The Bears began to wonder if the mysterious (and very cheeky) intruder might be upstairs. There was definitely no one downstairs, so they clambered up to the bedroom.

As soon as Papa Bear looked around the bedroom, he noticed his bed. Papa Bear cried out, in his usual deep, gruff, voice, "Someone's been sleeping in my bed!"

"Someone's been sleeping in MY bed," gasped Mama Bear.

Once again, it was Baby Bear's turn: "Someone's been sleeping in MY bed," he cried, "and she's STILL there!"

At the sound of Papa Bear's shouting, Mama Bear's gasping, and Baby Bear's crying, Goldilocks finally woke up. What a fright she had, too, when this mischievous little girl opened her eyes to see the three bears standing over her!

Goldilocks let out a high-pitched scream, leapt out of the bed and ran down the stairs and out of the house as fast as she could. Goldilocks ran and ran, worried that the Bears were close behind her.

Eventually, she made it home – and, of course, the Bear family hadn't chased her at all as they had been rather startled by the little girl with the curly locks, sleeping in their bedroom.

Back at home, Goldilocks told her mother about her adventure. By the time she had finished telling the story, Goldilocks realised how wrong she had been to enter the Bears' house. Her mother made her promise that she would never do such a thing again. This was one little girl who had learned her lesson – never again would she help herself to things that didn't belong to her!

18

Cinderella

A long time ago there lived a gentleman and his charming wife, who took great pride in raising their only daughter to be a good and well-behaved girl. The child was most obedient and loved her parents dearly.

Sadly, after a long illness, the little girl's mother died. Father and daughter were heart-broken for a very long time.

Many years later, when his daughter reached her fourteenth birthday, the father married once again. He had longed for a new bride to help care for his beloved daughter.

His second wife, however, was unfortunately quite different to the first. She was lazy, grumpy, no-one could please her, and she had two grown-up daughters of a similar nature.

Minutes after the wedding was over, the new wife began to show her temper. She could not bear her husband's beautiful daughter, who seemed like an angel compared with her own children. Within days the new wife ordered her stepdaughter to sleep in the cellar so that her own daughters had a bedroom of their own.

The stepmother made the young girl wash all the dishes, polish the tables and chairs, sweep the floor, and make the beds. But the worst job of all was sweeping the fireplace. Every day the little girl was covered in cinders, and she soon became known as 'Cinderella'. But poor Cinderella followed her orders without complaint, fearing her father would be scolded himself – it had become quite clear that his new wife ruled the house!

One day, it so happened that Cinderella's grumpy stepsisters
were invited to a grand ball at the royal palace. The girls were busy
preparing for the event; every moment was spent deciding which
gown and shoes they should wear.

Such excitement meant more work for Cinderella, though, as she
was forced to iron their dresses and fix their hair. The stepsisters
talked of nothing but their appearance: "I," said the eldest, "will look
simply stunning in my scarlet velvet dress." "And I," said the youngest,
"will look marvellous in my gold muslin wrap and with diamonds in
my hair!"

On the morning of the ball the stepsisters called to Cinderella for
her opinion of their dresses, for the girls knew she had a great deal
of wisdom in these matters. Cinderella gave them the best advice she
could, and even adjusted their head-dresses.

But while Cinderella was busy
dressing her sisters, they said to
her, snickering, "Would you not like
to go to the ball, Cinders?" Cinderella
knew they were laughing at her, as she
was still covered in dust and dirt from the morning's chores.

Now most girls would take their revenge and mess up the sisters'
hair, or tear their dress, but not Cinderella. The sweet-natured girl
simply chose to ignore them.

As the stepsisters drove off to the ball in their beautiful horse-
drawn carriage, Cinderella followed them with her eyes. When they
were out of sight, she sat down and began to cry.

To Cinderella's surprise, her fairy godmother appeared.
Now her fairy godmother had appeared only once before – when
Cinderella's mother had died. "Tell me, dear," said the fairy
godmother, "what troubles you so?"

"I wish, I wish," sobbed Cinderella, "I wish I could go to
the ball!"

"Well, as you are such a good girl," said the fairy godmother,
"you shall go! Now run into the garden and bring me a pumpkin."

Cinderella flew like lightning, and brought the finest pumpkin
she could find. Her godmother scooped out the inside, then she
struck it with her wand and the pumpkin instantly turned into a
golden coach.

Next the fairy godmother sent Cinderella outside to find seven field mice. Cinderella did as she was told, and the godmother touched each mouse with her wand – six of the mice turned into beautiful white horses, while the seventh turned into a driver for the coach!

The fairy godmother then said to Cinderella, "Well, my dear, is this not the finest coach, with the finest horses, and the finest driver to take you to the finest ball? Are you not delighted?"

"Yes," replied Cinderella, "but must I wear these filthy rags?"

The fairy godmother touched Cinderella with the wand, and her rags became a stunning gown.

Cinderella looked perfect. She had a beautiful jewelled necklace and bracelet, and she wore the most dainty glass slippers. The fairy godmother gave Cinderella strict instructions before letting her go to the ball: "No matter what happens, you must leave the palace by the time the clock strikes twelve. Should you stay a single minute longer, the coach will once again become a pumpkin, the horses will become mice and the fine clothes will be changed back into filthy rags."

Cinderella promised to do exactly as she was told, and off she went to the ball.

When Cinderella arrived, everyone at the palace was amazed at her beauty. The dancing and the music stopped, and everybody stared at this beautiful stranger. The Prince came forward, led her into the ballroom, and begged her to dance with him throughout the evening!

The King and Queen particularly admired Cinderella's elegance and great manners. As for the Prince, he soon discovered that Cinderella was as kind and good as she was beautiful, and he knew that she was the girl for him. As the evening wore on, a fine feast was served. But the Prince was so busy gazing at Cinderella, he did not eat a bite.

Cinderella seated herself near her sisters, paid them much attention, and offered them some of the treats the Prince had given her. The sisters were quite astonished at such fine manners from a lady whom they did not know (or so they thought!).

All too soon, this wonderful evening was to come to an end for poor Cinderella. While dancing with the Prince, she heard the clock striking twelve. Cinderella almost flew out of the ballroom.

The Prince followed quickly behind, but he could not catch her. After searching high and low throughout the palace gardens, the Prince had found nothing but one of her little glass slippers.

As she passed through the palace gates, poor Cinderella was once again wearing her ragged old dress, and she had to walk all the way home.

When Cinderella's sisters returned, they teased her with glowing stories of the ball. They told her of a beautiful and mysterious guest, and how she had dropped a tiny glass slipper that the Prince had picked up, announcing to everyone that if he could find the owner of the slipper he would marry her!

The next day a royal messenger took the slipper to all the homes in the land. When he arrived at Cinderella's house her two sisters tried to force the slipper on, but it was no use.

The sisters' feet were far too big! Then, Cinderella slowly stepped forward, "May I try the slipper, sir?"

The stepsisters roared with laughter, "You? You? Why you never even went to the ball, silly girl!"

Cinderella ignored her nasty sisters and held out her foot. The moment the royal messenger saw Cinderella's tiny and delicate foot, he knew the slipper would fit. The two sisters were amazed! They were even more amazed when Cinderella pulled out the other slipper from her pocket!

At that very moment, Cinderella's fairy godmother appeared.

She touched Cinderella's ragged
clothes with her magic wand, making
her appear as magnificently dressed as
the night before.

The two sisters finally realized that their very own
stepsister, Cinderella, was in fact the mysterious guest from the
ball. They threw themselves at her feet, begging for forgiveness
for the terrible way they had treated Cinderella. Being such a
caring and good girl, Cinderella hugged her sisters, and said that
she forgave them.

It was time for the hugs and tears to end, as the royal messenger insisted that Cinderella return with him to the palace. Cinderella and the Prince were reunited, and they couldn't take their eyes off each other.

The most beautiful wedding in the land took place a few days later, with Cinderella's proud father and stepsisters at her side. Even her evil stepmother managed a smile!

Little Red Riding Hood

There was once a little girl who lived with her parents in a cottage on the edge of a large forest.

Her father was a woodcutter, and each morning he would go deep into the forest where he worked all day long chopping down trees.

For her birthday one year, the little girl's grandmother made her a red cloak with a hood to match. The little girl wore her beautiful red cloak every time she went outside - and that is why she became known as Little Red Riding Hood.

One day when Little Red Riding Hood was playing in the garden, she heard her mother calling from the cottage.

"Your grandmother is not very well, and she has decided to stay in bed today. Perhaps you could take her something to cheer her up."

So together they packed a basket. They put in a freshly baked loaf of bread, some butter and a jar of strawberry jam.

Then Little Red Riding Hood laid a clean cloth on top of the basket, and she was ready to go to her grandmother's house.

Now Little Red Riding Hood's grandmother lived on the other side of the forest. So before she set off, her mother made the little girl promise never to stray from the path, and never to talk to strangers.

Little Red Riding Hood listened carefully, then off she went dressed in her special red cloak.

"Go straight to Grandmother's house, and remember to keep to the path!" her mother called as she watched her disappear into the forest.

Little Red Riding Hood was half way to her grandmother's when a big grey wolf stepped out from behind a tree.

"Good morning, my dear. What a simply lovely red cloak you have on!" said the wolf, doing his best to look friendly.

When Little Red Riding Hood heard this, she forgot what her mother had told her, and she began to talk to the wolf.

"My grandmother made it for my birthday," said the little girl politely. "She's ill in bed, and I'm going to cheer her up!"

"How very kind, my dear," smiled the wolf trying not to show his sharp teeth.

"And what have you got in your basket for Grandmother?" the wolf asked Little Red Riding Hood.

"Freshly baked bread, golden butter and her favourite strawberry jam," she replied.

"How simply delicious," said the wolf licking his lips.

Can you believe that at that very moment, the wicked wolf was planning to gobble up Little Red Riding Hood, and her grandmother too, if he had half a chance!

"Where does your grandmother live?" asked the wolf.

"Right at the end of this path on the far side of the forest," said Little Red Riding Hood as she walked along.

"Why not take some of these beautiful flowers to your grandmother?" suggested the wolf - for he was trying to delay Little Red Riding Hood as long as he could.

When the little girl saw the flowers growing by the path, she stopped at once and began to pick them.

Little Red Riding Hood was so busy, she never noticed the wolf bound off down the path towards her grandmother's house.

Perhaps the wolf knew a short cut through the trees, for in less time than it takes to tell, he was knocking on Grandmother's door.

"Who is it?" called the old lady from her bed.

"It's Little Red Riding Hood," whispered the wolf as softly as he could.

"Just lift up the latch and walk right in!" said the grandmother.

The big grey wolf rushed through the door, bounded into the bedroom and leapt onto Grandmother's bed.

When the poor old lady heard the wolf snarl, and saw his sharp pointed teeth, she threw back the bedclothes, jumped out of bed, ran outside and hid behind the woodshed.

Meanwhile, the wolf put on one of Grandmother's spare nightdresses and one of her frilly nightcaps. He even found a spare pair of glasses on a table by the bed.

"I feel these glasses suit me very well. I really do look like a grandmother!" and the wolf smiled as he admired himself in the mirror.

"When Red Riding Hood arrives, I shall gobble her up, and I'll eat her grandmother later!" and the wolf sniggered and snapped his teeth loudly.

Then he jumped into Grandmother's bed, and pulled the bedclothes up to his chin.

Before very long, Little Red Riding Hood came skipping up the path and knocked gently on her grandmother's door.

"Who is there?" croaked the wolf trying his best to sound like the old lady.

"It's Little Red Riding Hood come to cheer you up," the little girl replied.

"Just lift the latch and walk right in!" said the wolf.

"How strange grandmother sounds, perhaps she has a sore throat," Little Red Riding Hood thought.

"How are you feeling today?" the little girl asked as she tiptoed across her grandmother's room. But when the little girl put down her basket and flowers, she jumped back in surprise.

"Why Grandmother, what big ears you have!" she cried.

"All the better to hear you with!" said the wolf in a hoarse voice. "Come closer my dear!"

So Little Red Riding Hood stepped a little closer to her grandmother's bed.

"Why Grandmother, what big eyes you have!" said the little girl staring at the wolf in her grandmother's silver glasses.

"All the better to see you with!" grinned the wolf. "Come closer my dear!"

So Little Red Riding Hood took one more step forward, and looked very carefully at the wolf in her grandmother's nightdress and frilly nightcap.

"Why Grandmother, what big teeth you have!" gasped Little Red Riding Hood.

"All the better to EAT you with!" snarled the wolf as he leapt out of bed.

"You're not my grandmother!" yelled Little Red Riding Hood.

"Indeed I'm not," growled the wolf. "I'm the big bad wolf, and I'm going to gobble you up!"

When she heard that, Little Red Riding Hood ran out of the room screaming at the top of her voice, with the wolf close behind her.

As she rushed out of the front door, she fell right into the arms of her father, the woodcutter.

He had been chopping down trees nearby, along with some of the other woodsmen. When he heard Little Red Riding Hood's screams, and saw Grandmother peeping from behind the woodshed, he guessed that something was wrong.

"The wolf is going to gobble me up," shrieked the little girl. "Look! He's right behind me!"

When the woodcutter saw the wolf run out of Grandmother's front door, he grabbed his sharp axe, ready to chop off the wolf's head.

When the wolf saw the woodcutter, he trembled with fright, and ran for his life.

"That wicked wolf must have gobbled up poor Grandmother," sobbed Little Red Riding Hood.

"No he hasn't!" smiled the little girl's father. "There she is. She's been hiding behind the woodshed all the time."

How happy everyone felt. Grandmother was safe, and feeling much better in spite of her fright. Little Red Riding Hood was safe too, thanks to her brave father.

The wicked wolf was gone forever, and would never
return while the woodcutters were in the forest.

It was getting late so the woodcutters headed for home.
No doubt they would tell their children that night, how they
had chased a big bad wolf, who was dressed in a nightdress
and frilly nightcap!

With the wolf gone, Grandmother could go back inside her own little home again, and Little Red Riding Hood could unpack her basket at last.

In fact, grandmother felt so much better, she put on her favourite dress and made tea.

Little Red Riding Hood put the flowers she had picked in the middle of the table, then she set out the bread and butter, and the jar of strawberry jam.

They all sat down, and Grandmother gave them a slice or two of her delicious chocolate cake.

After tea, Little Red Riding Hood and her father waved Grandmother goodbye, then walked home side by side through the forest.

The Ugly Duckling

It was a warm day in summer, and a mother duck was sitting all by herself on her nest at the far end of a pond. She felt rather lonely, for it seemed to her that she'd been there for ever.

She could hardly wait for her ducklings to hatch out, then they could swim in the pond together.

At long last one of the eggs cracked open, and out popped a tiny duckling, then another and another. Before very long, there were six fluffy yellow ducklings doing their best to jump out of the nest.

The mother duck knew the moment she saw her downy ducklings, that they were the most beautiful babies she had ever seen. And she couldn't wait to show them off to the other birds on the pond.

Then she noticed that the biggest of her eggs hadn't hatched. So she settled down to keep the egg warm underneath her soft feathers.

While the mother duck waited, she watched her ducklings scurrying to and fro as they explored their new world.

"I do believe that the world is a great deal bigger than our pond," she quacked nodding her head wisely. "It stretches right up to the farmyard...and that's as far as it goes I think!"

It didn't take long before the big egg began to crack open,
and a large grey bird with a huge head and a long neck came
tumbling out of its shell.

"Oh my! Oh my!" quacked the mother duck.

"You don't look a bit like your brothers and sisters.
I'm not even sure that you are a duckling at all!"

As soon as the other six ducklings heard all the noise, they
scurried out of the reeds and gathered round the new arrival.

"What is it?" peeped the ducklings all together.

"Well!" said the mother duck with a sigh. "He does look rather funny, a bit strange, you might say."

"He's not like us!" cheeped the smallest of the six ducklings. Then the others joined in. "He's not even yellow!" "His head is too big!" "His feet are enormous!" "AND HE'S UGLY!"

"Now, that is not so," said the mother duck. "He's not ugly, he's just different!"

But sad to say, from that day on, the poor duckling became known as the Ugly Duckling.

Mother duck was eager to show off her newly hatched family, so she led them down to the pond for their first swim.

When they reached the water's edge, the ducklings plopped in one by one, and soon they were swimming round in the water.

"Don't you dare come near us!" the six yellow ducklings shouted to the Ugly Duckling as they bobbed up and down near their mother.

"Why, he's the best swimmer of you all!" quacked the mother duck. "He may look different, but one day, he'll outshine every one of you!"

After a while, the mother duck led her ducklings across the pond and into the farmyard.

The geese and the rest of the birds gathered round and stared when they saw the Ugly Duckling.

"What is that?" hissed the farmyard gander rudely.

"He's the biggest of my new ducklings," the mother duck replied.

"He's the ugliest!" crowed the cockerel at the top of his voice.

The Ugly Duckling's six brothers and sisters cheeped with laughter, and the rest of the farmyard birds joined in.

Everyone was so unkind, it made the poor Ugly Duckling feel very unhappy.

As the weeks went by, the ducklings and their mother spent more and more time in the farmyard. The Ugly Duckling was pecked and hassled all day long.

"They tease me because I'm so ugly," thought the Ugly Duckling as he ran away from the other birds.

One morning a girl from the farmhouse came into the yard to feed the poultry.

"Get out of my way, you ugly creature!" and she threw grain from her bucket at the Ugly Duckling.

The duckling was so shocked, he tumbled through the hedge, and landed upside-down in a field full of sharp corn stalks.

The sparrows and finches that were perching on the branches fluttered up into the sky with fright.

"Everyone I meet is frightened because of the way I look," sighed the Ugly Duckling. "It must be because I am so ugly. I shall go far from here and never come back again!"

So early next morning, he ran away from the cruel birds in the farmyard.

The Ugly Duckling travelled all day long. At last he came to a great open marsh where the wild ducks lived.

"You're not the prettiest of ducks!" quacked one of the drakes. "But you're welcome to stay here as long as you like," and away he flew.

Week after week the Ugly Duckling hid in the rushes all alone. Nobody bothered him, until one day, a hunting dog came sniffing round.

The wild ducks flew off at once. There were men on the marsh carrying guns, and the wild ducks knew not to stay.

When the hunting dog discovered the Ugly Duckling, he growled and bared his teeth, then he turned and ran off into the reeds.

"Even the dog thinks
I'm ugly," said the duckling.
"That is the reason he didn't bite me!"

It was autumn now, and the
weather was getting colder day
by day. It was time for the Ugly Duckling
to leave the marsh and find somewhere
away from the wind and the rain.

After a long search, he came upon a tumbledown cottage.
It looked quite empty, so the duckling squeezed through a hole
in the door where the wood had rotted away.

Once inside the cottage, he hid in a corner and fell fast asleep.

When the Ugly Duckling woke up the next morning, he was in for a surprise. An old woman lived there with her cat and her hen and she found the duckling as soon as it was light.

The old woman was delighted the duckling had come and she begged him to stay. She thought he would lay plenty of duck eggs for tea.

But her companions, the cat and the hen, had other ideas.

"I can catch mice! Can you?" snarled the cat. The Ugly Duckling shook his head.

"I can lay eggs! Can you?" clucked the hen. The Ugly Duckling shook his head again, for he had no idea how to lay an egg.

"The old woman will fatten you up and eat you for dinner, you ugly bird!" sneered both the cat and the hen.

Their bullying went on and on. So after a while, although winter had arrived, the Ugly Duckling knew he had to move on.

So early one morning, before anyone in the cottage was awake, he squeezed out of the door where the wood had rotted away.

As the duckling walked through the day, snowflakes began to fall. Then, at long last, he came to a quiet lake. And there he stayed all alone. By day he swam in the icy water, and when darkness fell he went to sleep in the hollow of an old tree.

One evening as the sun was setting,
and a mist was drifting across the lake, the
Ugly Duckling looked up and saw a flock of
beautiful birds passing overhead.

"How I wish I was one of those birds,
then I could fly away with them and be happy
for ever."

That night he stayed on the water dreaming of those wonderful
birds. But by morning the lake had turned to ice. The poor duckling
was frozen fast and couldn't move.

A farmer who happened to be passing by, freed the poor bird and
carried him home in his thick jacket.

The farmhouse kitchen was cosy and warm, and the Ugly
Duckling soon thawed out. The farmer's children were very young
and wanted to play with him. It seemed like fun to them.

But the Ugly Duckling didn't know they were just being friendly,
he was frightened and tried to get away.

He stumbled around the kitchen in panic, he knocked over the milk, fell into the flour and then ran across the butter.

The farmer's wife clapped her hands, the children screamed and the farmer chased him out of the door!

So the Ugly Duckling fled to the lake, and went back and hid in the hollow tree. He stayed there until the snow was gone and the ice had melted away.

Spring came at last! The weather was warm and sunny, and great flocks of birds returned to the lake. Winter was gone, and for the first time in his life the Ugly Duckling felt happy to be alive.

Boldly he swam into the middle of the lake, then he spread out his strong wings and soared high into the air...he could fly!

As he landed gracefully at the edge of the lake, he saw his reflection in the clear water. Looking back at him was a beautiful white bird.

He could hardly believe his eyes, for during the long months of winter, the Ugly Duckling had grown into a magnificent swan.

Very soon, the other swans on the lake came gliding across the water to make him welcome.

"Are you alone?" asked one of the swans in the kindest way.

"Please come and live with us," said another.

No words can ever describe how happy this made the beautiful new swan feel.

A little girl had come to the water's edge to feed the birds.
"Come quickly!" she called to her mother.

"There's a new swan on the lake today, and he's the loveliest of them all!"

The new swan's dreams had come true at last, and no one would ever call him ugly again.